Mrs Pearson, Richard Scrafton Sharpe

Dame Wiggins of Lee, and Her Seven Wonderful Cats

A humorous tale

Mrs Pearson, Richard Scrafton Sharpe

Dame Wiggins of Lee, and Her Seven Wonderful Cats
A humorous tale

ISBN/EAN: 9783337075859

Printed in Europe, USA, Canada, Australia, Japan

Cover: Foto ©Andreas Hilbeck / pixelio.de

More available books at **www.hansebooks.com**

DAME WIGGINS OF LEE,

AND HER

SEVEN WONDERFUL CATS:

A HUMOROUS TALE

WRITTEN PRINCIPALLY BY A LADY OF NINETY.

EDITED, WITH ADDITIONAL VERSES,

BY JOHN RUSKIN, LL.D.,

HONORARY STUDENT OF CHRIST CHURCH,
AND HONORARY FELLOW OF CORPUS CHRISTI COLLEGE, OXFORD.

AND WITH NEW ILLUSTRATIONS

BY KATE GREENAWAY.

WITH TWENTY-TWO WOODCUTS.

GEORGE ALLEN,
SUNNYSIDE, ORPINGTON, KENT.
1885.

Printed by Hazell, Watson, and Viney, Ld., London and Aylesbury.

PREFACE.

THE woodcuts which illustrate the following
nursery rhymes have been facsimiled with ex-
emplary care and admirable skill by Mr. W. H.
Hooper, from those which were given coloured
by hand in the edition of 1823. But I think
that clever children will like having the mere out-
lines to colour in their own way; and for older
students there may be some interest in observing
how much life and reality may be obtained by
the simplest methods of engraving, when the
design is founded on action instead of effect. The
vigorous black type of the text has also been
closely matched by the care of Messrs. Hazell.

I have spoken in 'Fors' (vol. v., pp. 37-8)
of the meritorious rhythmic cadence of the verses,
not, in its way, easily imitable. In the old book,
no account is given of what the cats learned

when they went to school, and I thought my younger readers might be glad of some notice of such particulars. I have added, therefore, the rhymes on the third, fourth, eighth, and ninth pages—the kindness of Miss Greenaway supplying the needful illustrations. But my rhymes do not ring like the real ones ; and I would not allow Miss Greenaway to subdue the grace of her first sketches to the formality of the earlier work : but we alike trust that the interpolation may not be thought to detract from the interest of the little book, which, for the rest, I have the greatest pleasure in commending to the indulgence of the Christmas fireside, because it relates nothing that is sad, and pourtrays nothing that is ugly.

J. RUSKIN.

4th October, 1885.

DAME WIGGINS OF LEE,

AND HER

SEVEN WONDERFUL CATS.

A HUMOUROUS TALE.

WRITTEN PRINCIPALLY BY A LADY OF NINETY.

EMBELLISHED WITH EIGHTEEN COLOURED ENGRAVINGS.

LONDON:

PRINTED FOR

A. K. NEWMAN & Co. LEADENHALL-STREET.

1823.

DAME WIGGINS of Lee
Was a worthy old soul,
As e'er threaded a nee-
dle, or wash'd in a bowl:
She held mice and rats
In such antipa-thy;
That seven fine cats
Kept Dame Wiggins of Lee.

The rats and mice scared
By this fierce whisker'd crew,
The poor seven cats
Soon had nothing to do;
So, as any one idle
She ne'er loved to see,
She sent them to school,
Did Dame Wiggins of Lee.

The Master soon wrote
That they all of them knew
How to read the word " milk "
And to spell the word " mew."
And they all washed their faces
Before they took tea :
' Were there ever such dears ! '
Said Dame Wiggins of Lee.

He had also thought well
To comply with their wish
To spend all their play-time
In learning to fish
For stitlings; they sent her
A present of three,
Which, fried, were a feast
For Dame Wiggins of Lee.

But soon she grew tired
Of living alone;
So she sent for her cats
From school to come home.
Each rowing a wherry,
Returning you see:
The frolic made merry
Dame Wiggins of Lee.

The Dame was quite pleas'd,
And ran out to market;
When she came back
They were mending the carpet.
The needle each handled
As brisk as a bee;
"Well done, my good cats,"
Said Dame Wiggins of Lee.

To give them a treat,
She ran out for some rice;
When she came back,
They were skating on ice.
"I shall soon see one down,
Aye, perhaps, two or three,
I'll bet half-a-crown,"
Said Dame Wiggins of Lee.

When spring-time came back
They had breakfast of curds;
And were greatly afraid
Of disturbing the birds.
"If you sit, like good cats,
All the seven in a tree,
They will teach you to sing!"
Said Dame Wiggins of Lee.

So they sat in a tree,
And said "Beautiful! Hark!"
And they listened and looked
In the clouds for the lark.
Then sang, by the fireside,
Symphonious-ly,
A song without words
To Dame Wiggins of Lee.

They called the next day
On the tomtit and sparrow,
And wheeled a poor sick lamb
Home in a barrow.
"You shall all have some sprats
For your humani-ty,
My seven good cats,"
Said Dame Wiggins of Lee.

While she ran to the field,
To look for its dam,
They were warming the bed
For the poor sick lamb :
They turn'd up the clothes
All as neat as could be ;
" I shall ne'er want a nurse,"
Said Dame Wiggins of Lee.

She wished them good night,
And went up to bed:
When, lo! in the morning,
The cats were all fled.
But soon—what a fuss!
"Where can they all be?
Here, pussy, puss, puss!"
Cried Dame Wiggins of Lee.

The Dame's heart was nigh broke,
So she sat down to weep,
When she saw them come back
Each riding a sheep:
She fondled and patted
Each purring Tom-my:
" Ah! welcome, my dears,"
Said Dame Wiggins of Lee.

The Dame was unable
Her pleasure to smother;
To see the sick Lamb
Jump up to its mother.
In spite of the gout,
And a pain in her knee,
She went dancing about:
Did Dame Wiggins of Lee.

The Farmer soon heard
Where his sheep went astray,
And arrived at Dame's door
With his faithful dog Tray.
He knocked with his crook,
And the stranger to see,
Out of window did look
Dame Wiggins of Lee.

For their kindness he had them
All drawn by his team;
And gave them some field-mice,
And raspberry-cream.
Said he, " All my stock
You shall presently see;
For I honour the cats
Of Dame Wiggins of Lee."

He sent his maid out
For some muffins and crumpets;
And when he turn'd round
They were blowing of trumpets.
Said he, "I suppose,
She's as deaf as can be,
Or this ne'er could be borne
By Dame Wiggins of Lee."

To show them his poultry,
He turn'd them all loose,
When each nimbly leap'd
On the back of a Goose,
Which frighten'd them so
That they ran to the sea,
And half-drown'd the poor cats
Of Dame Wiggins of Lee.

For the care of his lamb,
And their comical pranks,
He gave them a ham
And abundance of thanks.
" I wish you good-day,
My fine fellows," said he ;
" My compliments, pray,
To Dame Wiggins of Lee."

You see them arrived
At their Dame's welcome door;
They show her their presents,
And all their good store.
"Now come in to supper,
And sit down with me;
All welcome once more,"
Cried Dame Wiggins of Lee.